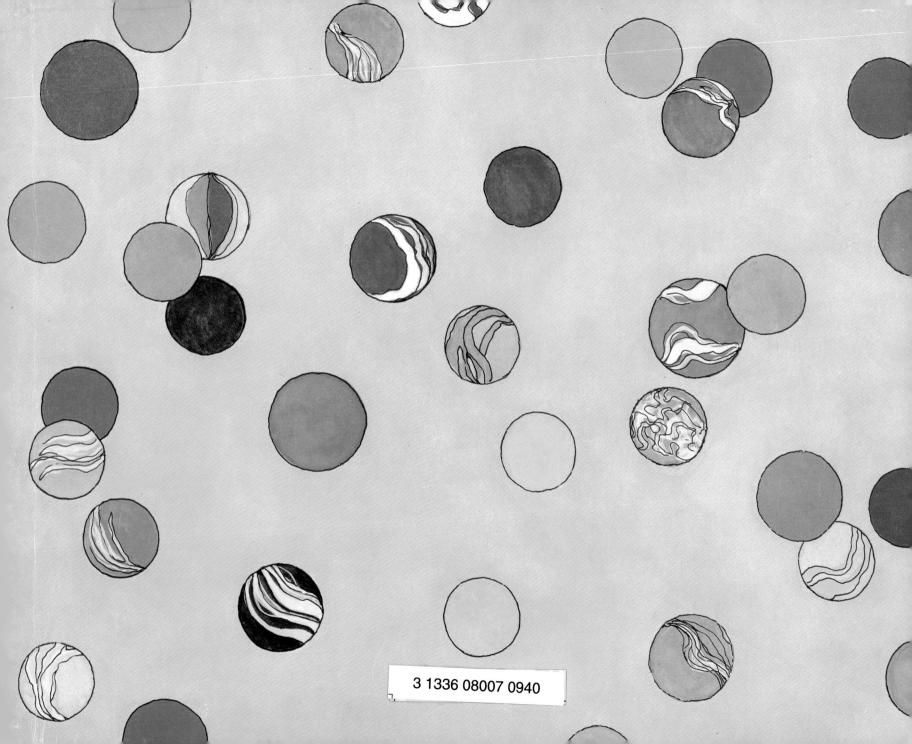

First published in the United States 1988 by
Dial Books for Young Readers
A Division of NAL Penguin Inc.
2 Park Avenue / New York, New York 10016
Published in Great Britain by The Bodley Head
Copyright © 1988 by Susanna Gretz / All rights reserved
Printed and bound in Great Britain
First Edition
(c)
1  2  3  4  5  6  7  8  9  10

Library of Congress Cataloging in Publication Data
Gretz, Susanna.
Roger loses his marbles / Susanna Gretz.
p.   cm.
Summary: When Aunt Lulu pays a visit, she stays in Roger's
room and tidies it up, which makes him mad
until she finds something that Roger lost.
ISBN 0-8037-0565-4
[1. Orderliness—Fiction. 2. Lost and found possessions—Fiction.
3. Pigs—Fiction.] I. Title.
PZ7.G8636Rj 1988   [E]—dc19   88-3753  CIP  AC

# Roger Loses His Marbles!

## Susanna Gretz

Dial Books for Young Readers / *New York*

Roger's aunt is coming to stay. It's her birthday.
Roger's dad, sister, mother, and uncle
are all getting ready for the party.

Roger, however, is looking for his yellow marbles.

"And don't put everything on the bed, Roger!" says his mother. "Aunt Lulu's going to sleep in your room."

*Ding-a-ling!* The doorbell rings.
"**Hurry up now, Roger,**" says Uncle Tim.
"**Aunt Lulu's** here."

Roger has to sleep in the baby's room!

"Oh my, what a pigpen!" says Aunt Lulu.

She gets right to work.
"I always put my suitcase under the bed," she says.

"Toys belong in the toy box,"
says Aunt Lulu.

"No!" yells Roger.
"Why not?" says Aunt Lulu.

"Because I always keep my *yellow marbles* in the bottom of the box."

"Well put them in then," says Aunt Lulu.

"But I can't find them!" says Roger in exasperation.

Just then the guests begin to arrive.
"Roger, dear," says his mother,
"please come and help."

Aunt Lulu is quite overcome.

"We'll clear up, Aunt Lulu," says Roger's dad.
"You trot along to bed."

But Aunt Lulu can't possibly go to bed yet.
There are still a few things to clean up . . .
one blue crayon . . .

a piece of Lego . . .

a bit of kite string.

Finally she gets into bed.
But what are *those* doing on the windowsill?

Aunt Lulu tiptoes in to find Roger.
"Look what I've found," she says.

They creep back into Roger's room.

"Wow, Aunt Lulu," says Roger. "You're not bad at marbles!"
"And your room's not bad for playing marbles in," says Aunt Lulu,

"... especially when it's clean!"

"Good night, Aunt Lulu," says Roger.

"Happy Birthday!"